Where's the ball?

Written by Tom Ottway

Illustrated by Victor Tavares

Collins

What's in this book?

Listen and say 🎧

shuttlecock

player

badminton

score

net

racket

 Julia said, "Let's play badminton."
Jaz said, "OK. Where's the ball, Julia?"
Julia said, "Good question! There isn't one!"
Zak said, "What?"

Jaz said, "How do we play?"

In badminton there isn't a ball.
You use a shuttlecock.

You hit the shuttlecock with the racket.

A shuttlecock has feathers and it goes very fast! It can travel at 300 (kmph) kilometres an hour. That's faster than a train.

whoosh

9

Badminton is an old game. It started in England. Here's a picture. The clothes are very different. The women are wearing dresses and the men are wearing trousers.

Badminton is for everyone: for young and old people all over the world. It's easy. You can play on the beach, in the park or in a sports centre.

This is Lin Dan. He is a famous badminton player. He is from China. He plays with his left hand, and he won two Olympic gold medals.

P.V. Sindhu is from India. She is a very famous player. She is very good at badminton and she makes a lot of money from playing. People love her!

serve

Each player has a badminton racket.
Player 1 hits the shuttlecock to Player 2.
This is called a serve.

Then Player 2 hits the shuttlecock to Player 1.

Player 1 didn't hit it! The shuttlecock is on the floor.

That's a point for Player 2.

Now Player 2 can serve. The players play the game.

The shuttlecock hits the net. So it's a point for Player 1. Player 2 isn't happy. Now Player 1 serves again. The score is 1–1.

19

When a player gets 21 points they are the winner.

Jaz and Zak have a good game. Zak gets 19 points, but Jaz gets 21 points. Jaz is the winner.

Zak said, "Let's play again!"

"OK!" said Jaz, "You can serve."

Picture dictionary

Listen and repeat

feather

medal

net

racket

score

Player 1 Player 2
0 : 0

serve

shuttlecock

1 Look and say "Yes" or "No".

2 Listen and say

Collins

Published by Collins
An imprint of HarperCollins*Publishers*
Westerhill Road
Bishopbriggs
Glasgow
G64 2QT

HarperCollins*Publishers*
1st Floor, Watermarque Building
Ringsend Road
Dublin 4
Ireland

William Collins' dream of knowledge for all began with the publication of his first book in 1819.

A self-educated mill worker, he not only enriched millions of lives, but also founded a flourishing publishing house. Today, staying true to this spirit, Collins books are packed with inspiration, innovation and practical expertise. They place you at the centre of a world of possibility and give you exactly what you need to explore it.

© HarperCollins*Publishers* Limited 2020

10 9 8 7 6 5 4 3 2

ISBN 978-0-00-839647-3

Collins® and COBUILD® are registered trademarks of HarperCollins*Publishers* Limited

www.collins.co.uk/elt

British Library Cataloguing in Publication Data

A catalogue record for this publication is available from the British Library.

Author: Tom Ottway
Illustrator: Victor Tavares (Beehive)
Series editor: Rebecca Adlard
Publishing manager: Lisa Todd
Product managers: Jennifer Hall and Caroline Green
In-house editor: Alma Puts Keren
Project manager: Emily Hooton
Editor: Frances Amrani
Proofreaders: Natalie Murray and Michael Lamb
Cover designer: Kevin Robbins
Typesetter: 2Hoots Publishing Services Ltd
Audio produced by id audio, London
Reading guide author: Emma Wilkinson
Production controller: Rachel Weaver
Printed and bound by: GPS Group, Slovenia

Download the audio for this book and a reading guide for parents and teachers at www.collins.co.uk/839647